THIS BOOK BELONGS TO :

_____

RhymeTimeDoodles

My Bubbe's Arms

Printed in Hong Kong

ISBN 1-886611-00-9
Library of Congress Catalog Card Number: 97-78201

Published by Atara Publishing, Stanton, California

ATARA PUBLISHING
http://www.doodles.com

I've always had a special place, a warm and cozy gentle space,

*W*here I can talk about my fears, where no one else can see my tears,

A secret place so safe from harm, cuddled in my Bubbe's arms.

I've never wanted fancy things, like shiny toys or silver rings,

I'd rather have
the magic charms
of being held close
in Bubbe's arms.

On winter days we like to walk, I listen to my Bubbe talk. I never think to stay inside for underneath her arms I'll hide.

*A*nd when the rain falls from the sky, my Bubbe's arms will keep me dry.

When she's sweeping with her broom, I follow her from room to room.

And Bubbe laughs,   for wherever she goes,

$\mathcal{I}$'m right there standing on her toes.

When the work is done we take a break, I'll have hot cocoa and some cake.

*B*ubbe drinks a cup of tea,
guess who's sitting on her knee? ME!

*O*ops! I spilled some on the rug,
Bubbe, quick, I need a hug!

Bubbe rocks me like a cradle,
singing to her shaine maidel.

Soon my eyes begin to close,
it won't be long before I doze.

And if a monster pokes its head
from underneath my little bed,

He'll never get
his chance to bite,
in Bubbe's arms
I'm gone from sight!

I wonder,
when I'm fully grown,
with a family
of my own,

*W*ill I be
too big or old
for my Bubbe's
arms to hold?

But Bubbe says
if I grow tall,
with feet that reach
from wall
to wall,

If I grow large from side to side,
if I'm a million inches wide,

I'll
never be
too big
or old,
for her arms
to hug
and hold.

I wonder...
Does my Bubbe see there's no place else
I'd rather be, than snuggled near my favorite part,
within her arms, close to her heart.